Chinese Graded Reader

Breakthrough Level: 150 Characters

我的老師是火星人
Wǒ de Lǎoshī Shì Huǒxīngrén

My Teacher Is a Martian

by Jared Turner and John Pasden

Mind Spark Press LLC

SHANGHAI

Published by Mind Spark Press LLC

Shanghai, China

Mandarin Companion is a trademark of Mind Spark Press LLC.

Copyright © Mind Spark Press LLC, 2019

For information about educational or bulk purchases, please contact Mind Spark Press at business@mandarincompanion.com.

Instructor and learner resources and traditional Chinese editions of the Mandarin Companion series are available at www.MandarinCompanion.com.

First paperback print edition 2020

Library of Congress Cataloging-in-Publication Data
Turner, Jared.

My Teacher Is a Martian : Mandarin Companion Graded Readers: Level 0, Simplified Chinese Edition / John Pasden and Jared Turner; [edited by] John Pasden, Chen Shishuang, Li Jiong, Ma Lihua

1st paperback edition.

Shanghai, China / Salt Lake City, UT: Mind Spark Press LLC, 2019

Library of Congress Control Number: 2019910036
ISBN: 9781941875490 (Paperback)
ISBN: 9781941875513 (Paperback/traditional ch)
ISBN: 9781941875506 (ebook)
ISBN: 9781941875520 (ebook/traditional ch)
MCID: TFH20200421T153029JT

All rights reserved; no part of this publication may be reproduced, stored in a retrieval system, transmitted in any form, or by any means, electronic, mechanical, photocopying, recording, or otherwise, without the prior written permission of the publishers.

Mandarin Companion Graded Readers

Now you can read books in Chinese that are fun and help accelerate language learning. Every book in the Mandarin Companion series is carefully written to use characters, words, and grammar that a learner is likely to know.

The Mandarin Companion Leveling System has been meticulously developed through an in-depth analysis of textbooks, education programs and natural Chinese language. Every story is written in a simple style that is fun and easy to understand so you improve with each book.

Mandarin Companion Breakthrough Level

The Breakthrough Level is intended for Chinese learners who have obtained a low elementary or novice level of Chinese. Most students will be able to approach this book after one year of traditional formal study, depending on the learner and program. In creating this story, we have carefully balanced the need for level-appropriate simplicity against the needs of the story's plot.

The Breakthrough Level is written using a core set of 150 characters, a subset of the 300 characters used in Mandarin Companion Level 1. This ensures that the vocabulary will be limited to simple, everyday words, composed of characters that the learner is most likely to know. Any new characters used outside of the 150 Breakthrough Level characters are exclusively borrowed from the Level 1 character set, meaning that with each new story, the reader is systematically building toward Level 1.

Key words that the reader is not likely to know are added gradually over the course of the story accompanied by a numbered footnote for each instance. Pinyin and an English definition are provided at the bottom of the page for the first instance of each key word, and a complete glossary is provided at the back of the book. All proper nouns have been underlined to help the reader distinguish between names and other words.

What level is right for me?

If you are able to comfortably read this book without looking up lots of words, then this book is likely at your level. It is ideal to have at most only one unknown word or character for every 40-50 words or characters that are read.

Once you are able to read fluidly and quickly without interruption you are ready for the next level. Even if you are able to understand all of the words in the book, we recommend that readers build fluidity and reading speed before moving to higher levels.

How will this help my Chinese?

Reading extensively in a language you are learning is one of the most effective ways to build fluency. However, the key is to read at a high level of comprehension. Reading at the appropriate level in Chinese will increase your speed of character recognition, help you to acquire vocabulary faster, teach you to naturally learn grammar, and train your brain to think in Chinese. It also makes learning Chinese more fun and enjoyable. You will experience the sense of accomplishment and confidence that only comes from reading entire books in Chinese.

Extensive Reading

After years of studying Chinese, many people ask, "why can't I become fluent in Chinese?" Fluency can only happen when the language enters our "comfort zone." This comfort comes after significant exposure to and experience with the language. The more times you meet a word, phrase, or grammar point the more readily it will enter your comfort zone.

In the world of language research, experts agree that learners can acquire new vocabulary through reading only if the overall text can be understood. Decades of research indicate that if we know approximately 98% of the words in a book, we can comfortably "pick up" the 2% that is unfamiliar. Reading at this 98% comprehension level is referred to as "extensive reading."

Research in extensive reading has shown that it accelerates vocabulary learning and helps the learner to naturally understand grammar. Perhaps most importantly, it trains the brain to automatically recognize familiar language, thereby freeing up mental energy to focus on meaning and ideas. As they build reading speed and fluency, learners will move from reading "word by word" to processing "chunks of language." A defining feature is that it's less painful than the "intensive reading" commonly used in textbooks. In fact, extensive reading can be downright fun.

Graded Readers

Graded readers are the best books for learners to "extensively" read. Research has taught us that learners need to "encounter" a word 10-30 times before truly learning it, and often many more times for particularly complicated or abstract words. Graded readers are appropriate for learners because the language is controlled and simplified, as opposed to the language in native texts, which is inevitably difficult and often demotivating. Reading extensively with graded readers allows learners to bring together all of the language they have studied and absorb how the words naturally work together.

To become fluent, learners must not only understand the meaning of a word, but also understand its nuances, how to use it in conversation, how to pair it with other words, where it fits into natural word order, and how it is used in grammar structures. No textbook could ever be written to teach all of this explicitly. When used properly, a textbook introduces the language and provides the basic meanings, while graded readers consolidate, strengthen, and deepen understanding.

Without graded readers, learners would have to study dictionaries, textbooks, sample dialogs, and simple conversations until they have randomly encountered enough Chinese for it to enter their comfort zones. With proper use of graded readers, learners can tackle this issue and develop greater fluency now, at their current levels, instead of waiting until some period in the distant future. With a stronger foundation and greater confidence at their current levels, learners are encouraged and motivated to continue their Chinese studies to even greater heights. Plus, they'll quickly learn that reading Chinese is fun!

About Mandarin Companion

Mandarin Companion was started by Jared Turner and John Pasden who met one fateful day on a bus in Shanghai when the only remaining seat left them sitting next to each other. A year later, Jared had greatly improved his Chinese using extensive reading but was frustrated at the lack of suitable reading materials. He approached John with the prospect of creating their own series. Having worked in Chinese education for nearly a decade, John was intrigued with the idea and thus began the Mandarin Companion series.

John majored in Japanese in college, but started learning Mandarin and later moved to China where his learning accelerated. After developing language proficiency, he was admitted into an all-Chinese masters program in applied linguistics at East China Normal University in Shanghai. Throughout his learning process, John developed an open mind to different learning styles and a tendency to challenge conventional wisdom in the field of teaching Chinese. He has since worked at ChinesePod as academic director and host, and opened his own consultancy, AllSet Learning, in Shanghai to help individuals acquire Chinese language proficiency. He lives in Shanghai with his wife and children.

After graduate school and with no Chinese language skills, Jared decided to move to China with his young family in search of career opportunities. Later while working on an investment project, Jared learned about extensive reading and decided that if it was as effective as it claimed to be, it could help him learn Chinese. In three months, he read 10 Chinese graded readers and his language ability quickly improved from speaking words and phrases to a conversational level. Jared has an MBA from Purdue University and a bachelor in Economics from the University of Utah. He lives in Shanghai with his wife and children.

Credits

Original Author: Jared Turner

Story Authors: John Pasden, Jared Turner

Editor-in-Chief: John Pasden

Content Editor: Chen Shishuang

Editors: Li Jiong, Ma Lihua

Illustrator: Hu Sheng

Producer: Jared Turner

Acknowledgments

We are grateful to Ma Lihua, Li Jiong, Song Shen, Tan Rong, Chen Shishuang, and the entire team at AllSet Learning for working on this project and contributing the perfect mix of talent to produce this series.

Special thanks to Wang Hui and her 7th grade Chinese dual immersion class at Adele C. Young Intermediate School for being our test readers: AJ Bushnell, Brandon Murray, Colin Grunander, Emma Page, Isaak Diehl, Jackson Faerber, Jason Lee, Kyden Cefalo, Max Norton, Maxwell Isaacson, Olivia Barker, and Xavier Putnam. Also thanks to Jake Liu, Paris Yamamoto, Rory O'Neill, and Miles Turner for being our test readers.

Table of Contents

	i	Story Adaptation Notes
	ii	Characters
	iii	Locations
1		**Chapter 1** 外星人
6		**Chapter 2** 車老師
11		**Chapter 3** 他是人嗎？
16		**Chapter 4** 車老師的家
20		**Chapter 5** 很大的星星
24		**Chapter 6** 方老師
29		**Chapter 7** 本子
34		**Chapter 8** 不認識的字
39		**Chapter 9** 車老師走了
43		**Chapter 10** 水老師
48		Key Words
55		Appendix A: Character Comparison Reference
59		Appendix B: Grammar Points
61		Other Stories from Mandarin Companion

Story Adaptation Notes

Any learner that has managed to learn 150 Chinese characters knows it is not an easy task, and the prospect of reading a real text in Chinese seems discouragingly far-off. Typically textbook dialogs are the only reading material available for years on end. That's why being able to read an actual story with only 150 Chinese characters is a very big deal, and a huge help to the fluency development of early-stage learners.

The stories told at this 150-character Breakthrough Level are special, however. Nouns, verbs and adjectives at this level are in short supply, and the stories revolve around the limited vocabulary by necessity. This is why Breakthrough Level stories are not adaptations of western classics. They are original stories co-written by John Pasden and Jared Turner, specifically designed to be engaging to readers despite the limitations.

When John and Jared were generating story ideas at the Breakthrough Level, the character for "fire," 火 (huǒ), and for "star," 星 (xīng), were on a sheet of possible characters to be used. Together, these characters form the Chinese word for Mars: 火星 (Huǒxīng), which ignited an ambition to create a sci-fi story using the Chinese name of the fourth planet in our solar system. Jared recalled reading a story called "My Teacher is an Alien" in his youth, which provided the inspiration for a story about two Chinese elementary school students who suspect their teacher is, in fact, from Mars. From this spark of an idea, the Mandarin Companion story *My Teacher is a Martian* was born. For those who can read this book at an enjoyable pace, you are already well on your way towards progressing to the Level 1 stories.

P.S. There are two "Mandarin Companion Universe" and two sci-fi easter eggs hidden in the illustrations of this book. Can you find them?

Cast of Characters

謝心月
(Xiè Xīnyuè)

馬天明
(Mǎ Tiānmíng)

車老師
(Chē Lǎoshī)

方老師
(Fāng Lǎoshī)

水老師
(Shuǐ Lǎoshī)

Locations

山東 (Shāndōng)

Although not explicitly stated, this story takes place in a smallish city in China's Shandong Province.

Chapter 1
外星人

謝心月今年十歲，她是一個小學生。她有一個新朋友，叫"馬天明"，馬天明今年也是十歲。他們每天都一起去上學。

馬天明的爸爸今年已經四十歲了，他寫過很多書，他的新書裡有外星人，馬天明和謝心月都會看他寫的書。有時候，兩個爸爸會和他們一起

---

1 歲 (suì) *mw.* years old
2 小學生 (xiǎoxuéshēng) *n.* elementary school student
3 新 (xīn) *adj.* new
4 叫 (jiào) *v.* to be called, to call; to tell (someone to do something)
5 一起 (yīqǐ) *adv.* together
6 上學 (shàngxué) *vo.* to start school, to go to school
7 已經 (yǐjing) *adv.* already
8 外星人 (wàixīngrén) *n.* alien
9 有時候 (yǒu shíhou) *phrase* sometimes

去山上 看星星。

"有很多星星,可是 星星 太小了,星星 上有外星人 嗎?"馬天明 問謝心月。

"我也不知道。我很想見見外星人!"謝心月 說。

10 山上 (shānshàng) *phrase* on the mountain(s)
11 星星 (xīngxing) *n.* star, stars
12 可是 (kěshì) *conj.* but

"你不怕外星人嗎?"馬天明問。

"我不怕,你呢?"謝心月說。

馬天明說:"我也不怕。我爸爸說,外星人在天上可以看見我們,可是,我們不能看見他們。"

"我看了你爸爸寫的新書,書裡說了外星人的樣子。他是不是已經見過外星人了?"謝心月問。

馬天明笑了:"他沒有見過外星人。"

"你說,外星人會說中文嗎?"謝心月問。"要是他們不會說中文,我們怎麼和他們說話?"

13 怕 (pà) *v.* to be afraid (of)
14 天上 (tiānshàng) *n.* in the sky
15 看見 (kànjian) *vc.* to see
16 見過 (jiàn guo) *phrase* have met before
17 笑 (xiào) *v.* to laugh, to smile
18 要是 (yàoshi) *conj.* if
19 怎麼 (zěnme) *adv.* how
20 說話 (shuōhuà) *vo.* to speak (words), to talk

馬天明想了想說:"我不知道,可能他們可以。"

"要是你見了一個會說中文的外星人,你會跟他說什麼?"謝心月又問。

馬天明有很多話想問外星人,說:"我……我要問他們,他們的家在什麼地方,他們那裡和我們這裡有什麼不一樣,他們為什麼要來我們這裡……"

馬爸爸聽完以後就笑了。

"明天星期一,又要上學了。不知道外星人小朋友是不是也都要上學?"

21 想了想 (xiǎng le xiǎng) *phrase* thought about it for a second
22 可能 (kěnéng) *adv.; aux* maybe, possibly; possible
23 又 (yòu) *adv.* again
24 家 (jiā) *mw., n.* measure word for shops; home
25 地方 (dìfang) *n.* place
26 不一樣 (bù yīyàng) *phrase* not the same
27 聽 (tīng) *v.* to listen (to)
28 以後 (yǐhòu) *adv.* after; later, in the future
29 就 (jiù) *adv.* just
30 星期一 (Xīngqīyī) *tn.* Monday
31 小朋友 (xiǎopéngyou) *n.* kid

謝心月 說。

"見到外星人 的時候,你就 問他們 吧。"馬爸爸笑 了笑。

32 的時候 (de shíhou) *phrase* when…

Chapter 2
車老師

第二天，來了一個小學 老師，是男老師。"大家 好，我是你們的新 老師，你們可以叫 我車老師，我今年三十歲。"

"車？我沒有聽 過。"謝心月 說。

"我也沒聽 過。"馬天明 說，"車老師，你是哪裡人？"

"我去過很多地方，你問我是哪裡人，我不知道怎麼 說。"

老師的話有一點 好笑，學生們都笑了。

33 第二天 (dì-èr tiān) *phrase* the second day
34 小學 (xiǎoxué) *n.* elementary school
35 大家 (dàjiā) *n.* everyone
36 有一點 (yǒu yīdiǎn) *phrase* to be a little (too)
37 好笑 (hǎoxiào) *adj.* funny

車老師看過很多星星和火星的書,每次說到火星,他就能說很多:知道火星在哪裡,火星上沒有水,也沒有人……聽車老師說火星的時候,馬天明和謝心月都很開心。

38 火星 (Huǒxīng) *pn.* Mars
39 每次 (měi cì) *phrase* every time
40 開心 (kāixīn) *adj.* happy

"老師，你的家不在火星上，怎麼知道這麼多？"謝心月問。

"我爸爸的新書裡也沒寫過這麼多。"馬天明也說。

車老師沒說話，對他們笑笑。

有一天，學生和老師已經都走了，馬天明和謝心月回來拿東西。到門邊的時候，他們看到車老師在裡面。他一邊用左手寫字，一邊用右手寫字，一邊看書！

"快看，車老師！怎麼可能……"馬天明對謝心月說。

41 這麼 (zhème) *adv.* so…
42 有一天 (yǒu yī tiān) *phrase* one day…
43 回來 (huílai) *vc.* to come back
44 拿 (ná) *v.* to get, to hold
45 東西 (dōngxi) *n.* thing(s), stuff
46 門邊 (mén biān) *phrase* by the door
47 看到 (kàndào) *vc.* to see
48 裡面 (lǐmiàn) *n.* inside
49 一邊 (yībiān) *conj.* while doing… (two things)
50 看書 (kànshū) *vo.* to read, to study

謝心月 說："我看到 了，這不是我第一次 看到 他這樣 了。"

馬天明 又 說："車老師 是……是個 什麼人？"

"他會聽到 的！我們回家 說吧。"

51 第一次 (dì-yī cì) *phrase* first time
52 這樣 (zhèyàng) *pr.* like this
53 聽到 (tīngdào) *vc.* to hear
54 回家 (huíjiā) *vo.* to go home

謝心月 說。

第二天 中午 吃飯的時候，馬天明 對謝心月 說："我們快去問問他吧。他是我們的老師，他是一個好老師。"

"你去問吧，我不想去。"謝心月 說。

馬天明 笑笑："快去吧！車老師 是很好的人。"

謝心月 想了想："好吧，車老師 一個人在那兒吃飯。我們過去 吧。"

---

55 中午 (zhōngwǔ) *n.* noon
56 一個人 (yī gè rén) *phrase* alone
57 過去 (guòqu) *vc.* to go over

Chapter 3
他是人嗎？

謝心月和馬天明走到車老師的後面，車老師沒有看到他們。

看到車老師的飯很多，還沒吃，謝心月對馬天明說："老師的飯是不是不太好吃？我去拿我們的飯來一起吃吧。"

她一邊說，一邊去拿飯。

"我們不是來和老師吃飯的……"馬天明回頭叫她。

車老師聽到後面有人，回頭看到

---

58 後面 (hòumian) *n.* behind
59 還 (hái) *adv.* still
60 好吃 (hǎochī) *adj.* tasty
61 回頭 (huítóu) *vo.* to turn one's head

了馬天明。

"老師好。"

"你吃飯了嗎?"

"我們還沒有吃飯,我看到老師你也沒吃……"馬天明的話沒說完,車老師的飯都已經吃完了!

這時候,謝心月回來了,手裡拿的是她和馬天明的飯。

"我已經吃完了,你們吃吧。"車老師走的時候,對他們笑笑。

"這怎麼可能……那麼多飯,一下子

62 說完 (shuō wán) *vc.* to finish speaking
63 吃完 (chī wán) *vc.* to finish eating
64 這時候 (zhè shíhou) *phrase* at this time
65 手裡 (shǒu lǐ) *phrase* in one's hand

66 那麼 (nàme) *adv.* so…
67 一下子 (yīxiàzi) *adv.* all of a sudden; all at once

都沒了!"謝心月說。可是馬天明也不知道,他們都不知道車老師是怎麼吃完的。

"車老師是外星來的……"馬天明一邊吃一邊說。

"車老師和我們一樣，和我們說一樣的話，怎麼可能是外星人？"謝心月說。

馬天明還在吃："可是，你也看到了，他一邊用左手寫字，一邊用右手寫字，一邊看書。我想他是外星人吧。"

馬天明吃完了說："我也不知道。要是我們能到他家去看看，可能會知道為什麼。你要不要一起去？"

"你知道車老師的家在什麼地方嗎？"謝心月問。

馬天明說："我知道！"

謝心月很開心："好！馬天明，我

68 一樣 (yīyàng) *n.* the same　　69 看看 (kànkan) *v.* to take a look

和你一起去。"

Chapter 4
車老師的家

第二天 下午五點，馬天明 說："謝心月，我看見 車老師 已經 走了。我們在他後面，要小心 一點，不要說話。"

"好的，我知道了。"

他們在車老師 後面 走了一個多小時，謝心月 問："馬天明，這是去車老師家 的路嗎？怎麼 還 沒到……"

"這是車老師 回家 的路，快到車老師家 了。"馬天明 回頭 對謝心月 說。

可是，馬天明的話說完 的時候，車老師

---

70 小心 (xiǎoxīn) *v.* to be careful   71 小時 (xiǎoshí) *n.* hour

就不見了。

"人呢?怎麼一下子不見了?"馬天明說。

"車老師是不是已經看到我們了?我們這樣不太好吧。"謝心月聽起來有一點不開心。

"他不可能看到我們。我們小心一點,可能他已經到家了。你看,他的家在前面。"馬天明說。

"家裡沒人……"到了車老師家門邊,馬天明說。

"可能他去朋友家了吧。我們明天

---

72 不見了 (bùjiàn le) *phrase* disappeared
73 聽起來 (tīng qǐlai) *vc.* to sound…
74 不開心 (bù kāixīn) *phrase* not happy, to be unhappy
75 不可能 (bù kěnéng) *phrase* impossible (to)

再 來吧。"謝心月 說。

馬天明 還是 想 看到 車老師:"再看看,可能 他還 在路上。"

可是,一個小時 以後,車老師 還是 沒有回來。

76 再 (zài) *adv.* again (in the future)

77 路上 (lùshang) *n.* on the road, on the way

"都七點了,我們回家吧。"謝心月說。

"好,那我們明天再來。"

第三天下午,他們又小心地走在了車老師後面。可是,不知道怎麼了,車老師在路上又不見了。他們小心地走到車老師家,可是,他也沒有回家。

後來,他們又在車老師後面走了幾次,每次車老師都不見了,也不在他家裡。車老師每天回家以後去了哪裡呢?

---

78 小心地 (xiǎoxīn de) *phrase* carefully
79 怎麼了 (zěnme le) *phrase* what happened, what's the matter
80 次 (cì) *mw.* time(s)

Chapter 5
很大的星星

"馬天明，我們這樣 在車老師 後面 一個多星期 了，還是 什麼都不知道。" 謝心月 說。

馬天明 沒聽 謝心月 說話："馬上 到 車老師 家 了，我們就 去他家 門邊 吧。"

這時候，謝心月 看看 天，說："馬天明，快看！這裡有一個很大的星星！"

馬天明 也看看 天，說："怎麼會 這樣？你看！車老師 家 上面 的天有這麼 大的 星星……"

81 一個多星期 (yī gè duō xīngqī) *phrase* over a week
82 馬上 (mǎshàng) *adv.* right away
83 怎麼會 (zěnme huì) *phrase* how could
84 上面 (shàngmian) *n.* on, on top, above

他們說話的時候,走到了車老師家門邊。

謝月心說:"車老師的家在大星星的下面,可是車老師不在家裡。我們在他後面這麼多天了,他每天都不回家……"

85 下面 (xiàmian) *n.* below, under

馬天明還在看天。

他說："外星人的家不會在這裡，可是……"不能開門去看，馬天明很不開心。"我想去看看。"

"你不怕嗎？"謝心月說問。

"我不怕。"馬天明說。

"我也不怕。我可以叫我爸爸……來開這個門，他什麼門都會開。"謝心月說。

"這樣不好。再說，我們還不知道車老師是什麼人，不能跟你爸爸說。"馬天明說。

"那我們能和誰說？"

---

86 開門 (kāimén) *vo.* to open the door　　87 再說 (zàishuō) *conj.* furthermore, besides

"我們去跟方老師說吧，車老師家的上面有一個很大的星星，方老師是一個好老師，可能她會和我們來車老師的家看看。"

"好，那我們明天跟她說。"

Chapter 6
方老師

第二天下午,謝心月和馬天明問方老師:"老師,你有沒有去過車老師的家?"

"沒去過,怎麼了?"方老師笑了一下,"大家都走了,你們兩個怎麼還不回家?"

"我們知道車老師的家在哪兒。"謝心月說。

"你能不能和我們一起去車老師的家看看。"馬天明很小心地說,他們三個人可以聽見。

88 一下 (yīxià) *adv.* briefly, for a second 89 聽見 (tīngjiàn) *vc.* to hear

方老師 想了想，說，"車老師 怎麼了？你們為什麼要去他家？"

"車老師……他不是人……"馬天明 說每一個字都很小心。

"你說什麼？"方老師 聽起來 有一點生氣，"你是不是要說，車老師 不是一個好老師？"

"不是，他是一個好老師，可是，他和我們不一樣。"馬天明 說。

"有什麼不一樣？"方老師 問。

"他是火星 來的。"謝心月 不小心 跟方老師 說了。"我們在他後面 幾次。可是，他在路上 每次 都會一下子 不見了。"

90 生氣 (shēngqì) *vo., adj.* to get angry; angry

91 不小心 (bù xiǎoxīn) *phrase* to not be careful; accidentally

"我們每次去他家,他都不在家。你和我們一起去看看,好不好?"馬天明又說。

"他家上面有一個星星,星星也很大。我們這裡的天上沒有,我家,馬天明家上面也沒有。"謝心月又說。

"怎麼會 有那麼 大的星星?"方老師想。

"好吧。那我和你們去看看。"兩個 小朋友 說的話 有一點 好笑,可是,方老師 還是 去了。

到了車老師 家 門邊,他們看見 裡面有人。

"車老師 在家……"謝心月 看看 馬天明。

"車老師 在家 看書……? 怎麼 可能……?"馬天明 看看 謝心月,"他知道我們要來。"

謝心月 說:"可是,他怎麼會 知道我們要來?"

馬天明 又 看看 天:"怎麼會 這樣?

天上 的大星星 沒有了。"

"好了,我不知道你們兩個在車老師家 看到 過什麼。可是,我看到 車老師在家,以後 不要再 說他是火星人 了。"

方老師 有一點 生氣,"快回家 吧。"

92 好了 (hǎo le) *phrase* done　　93 火星人 (Huǒxīng-rén) *pn.* Martian

Chapter 7
本子

那天以後，馬天明和謝心月就不再去車老師家了。可是，他們還是每天都在說車老師。

"馬天明，我看到車老師手裡有一個本子，他每天都在上面寫東西。"

"什麼本子？"

"有一次，我們看到他一邊用左手寫字，一邊用右手寫字，一邊看書，對不對？寫字的那個本子和他每天拿的本子是一樣的。"

94 那天 (nà tiān) *tn.* that day
95 本子 (běnzi) *n.* notebook
96 一次 (yīcì) *phrase* one time

"你看過那個本子上寫的東西嗎?"馬天明問。

"沒有。那個本子在他手裡。我拿不到那個本子,沒有看過本子裡的字。"謝心月說。

"不用拿到那個本子，我們也可以看到。"馬天明笑了一下。

謝心月很開心："那，本子在哪裡呢？"

馬天明想了想："聽說，今天下午有很多老師不在，車老師也可能不在。他出去的時候，我們可以看看他的本子裡面寫了什麼。"

"你說得對。"謝心月說。

下午三點多的時候，車老師出去了，他沒有拿那個本子。學生們有的在看書，有的在寫字。

---

97 拿到 (nádào) *vc.* to get, to manage to get

98 聽說 (tīngshuō) *v.* to hear tell, to hear said (that)

99 出去 (chūqu) *vc.* to go out

馬天明和謝心月很開心,可是,他們不想大家知道他們要去看老師的東西。

"謝心月,"馬天明一邊叫他的朋友,一邊看車老師的本子。"我的本子在老師那裡,我去看看。"

"我的本子也在老師那裡。"說完,謝心月和馬天明一起走了過去。

"這麼多本子,哪個是我的?"謝心月在看學生們的本子,馬天明在看車老師的本子。

Chapter 8
不認識的字

車老師的本子上寫了很多字,可是,馬天明不認識本子上的字。"你見過這樣的字嗎?"馬天明說話的時候很小心,不想大家聽到。

"沒見過。車老師怎麼會寫這樣的字?這會不會是外星人的字?"

謝心月拿了幾個學生的本子,可是,她看的是車老師的本子。

"很有可能。"馬天明說。"我們都認識字。可是,他寫外星人的字,外星人認識,我們不認識。"

100 認識 (rènshi) *v.* to recognize

謝心月 點點頭，問："你看完了嗎？一會兒 車老師 回來 看到 我們，他會不開心 的。"

"這是什麼？"本子 上有一個人，這個人的頭裡面 有一個人，心裡面 還有一個人。外星人 不好看，可是 他們看起來 很開心。外星人 的手裡 還 拿了很多東西。

"馬天明！"謝心月 叫 了出來。"快看！怎麼會 有這樣 的東西？"

"小心 一點，不要叫，也不要怕。"馬天明 說。

謝心月 小心地 說，"去跟方老師 說

---

101 點點頭 (diǎndian tóu) *phrase* to (briefly) nod one's head
102 一會兒 (yīhuìr) *tn.* a little while
103 好看 (hǎokàn) *adj.* good-looking
104 看起來 (kàn qǐlai) *vc.* to look…
105 出來 (chūlai) *vc.* to come out

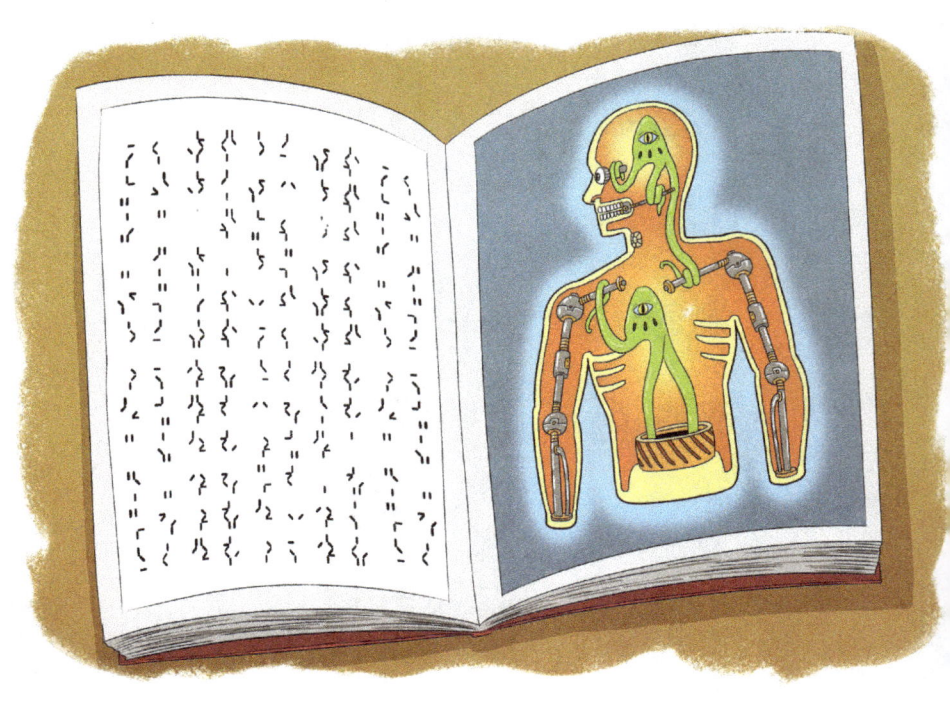

吧。"

他們去見了方老師。方老師 看到了他們,還 看到 了車老師 的本子。

方老師 說:"你們怎麼 有車老師 的本子?"

"方老師,車老師 的本子……裡面

寫的字我們都不認識,還有……你快看一下吧。"馬天明說。

"你們兩個怎麼還在說車老師?"方老師拿起那個本子,看了看,說:"你們要我看什麼?裡面什麼都沒有。"

"不可能!"馬天明和謝心月一起

說。馬天明拿起本子，說："我們都看到了，有很多外星人的字，還有外星人在一個人裡面⋯⋯"

"怎麼都沒有了？我不知道怎麼會這樣⋯⋯"謝心月有一點不開心。

"你們兩個，我也不知道說什麼了。"方老師說。

Chapter 9
車老師走了

一天中午吃飯的時候，謝心月問馬天明："你說，車老師是不是知道了？"

"有可能。"馬天明一邊吃飯，一邊說。

又過了幾個月，他們聽說車老師要走了，兩個人都不太開心。他們都知道車老師是外星人，可是，很多人都不知道。

"你說，車老師為什麼要走？"謝心月問馬天明。

106 幾個月 (jǐ gè yuè) *phrase* several months

馬天明想了想說:"車老師想,可能我們都知道他是外星人了。"

"也有可能是他要回火星了吧。"

謝心月笑了一下,"我也想和他一起去火星看看!"

馬天明說:"我想我們去了火星

以後，就不能回來了。"

说完，兩個人都笑了。

車老師走的那天，謝心月和馬天明拿到了車老師的那個本子。

"這是我的本子，給你們吧。"車老師說。

馬天明 和謝心月 一起 說:"謝謝老師。"

車老師 很開心地 說:"我還是 你們的朋友。再見!"

馬天明 和謝心月 不太開心:"老師再見!"

車老師 走的時候,誰都沒有問他要去哪兒,以後還 會不會回來。

"馬天明,本子 上寫的東西 都沒了。"謝心月 看完以後 說。

107 開心地 (kāixīn de) *phrase* happily

Chapter 10
水老師

車老師走了以後的第二年，又來了一個新的男老師。

"大家好，我是水老師，今年三十二歲。"男老師說，"我是你們今年的新老師，很開心認識大家。"

"水？"一個男生笑了，"我沒聽過。"

"我想，下一個老師會叫火老師。"馬天明也笑了。大家聽他這樣說，也都笑了。

---

108 第二年 (dì-èr nián) *phrase* second year
109 男生 (nánshēng) *n.* boy, male student
110 下一個 (xià yī ge) *phrase* next (one)

馬天明 和謝心月 沒想到 的是,水老師 和車老師 一樣,也看過很多星星 和火星 的書。每次 說到火星,水老師 也會說 很多。

"水老師,你知道嗎?"謝心月 說,"去

111 沒想到 (méi xiǎngdào) *phrase* to never have imagined

年我們有一個車老師。他和你一樣,每次說到火星,也會說很多。"

"水老師,你可能不認識他。"馬天明說。"他……很不一樣。"

"怎麼不一樣?"水老師一邊笑一邊問。

"他很喜歡星星,很喜歡火星。"馬天明說。

"我也是!"水老師說。"我認識車老師。他是我的好朋友。"

"你也是?那,你也是火星人?"馬天明問。

水老師說:"他和我說過你們。他說

你們喜歡去他家,說你們也喜歡看他的本子。"

"他都知道!"謝心月說。

"你們還有他的本子嗎?"水老師問。

"你要這個本子嗎?"馬天明不開心。

"我不要。"水老師說。"車老師已經給你們了。"

"可是本子上面沒有字了!"謝心月說。

"以後會有的。"水老師說。"會有的。"

Key Words 關鍵詞 (Guānjiàncí)

1. 歲 (suì) *mw.* years old
2. 小學生 (xiǎoxuéshēng) *n.* elementary school student
3. 新 (xīn) *adj.* new
4. 叫 (jiào) *v.* to be called, to call; to tell (someone to do something)
5. 一起 (yīqǐ) *adv.* together
6. 上學 (shàngxué) *vo.* to start school, to go to school
7. 已經 (yǐjing) *adv.* already
8. 外星人 (wàixīngrén) *n.* alien
9. 有時候 (yǒu shíhou) *phrase* sometimes
10. 山上 (shānshàng) *phrase* on the mountain(s)
11. 星星 (xīngxing) *n.* star, stars
12. 可是 (kěshì) *conj.* but
13. 怕 (pà) *v.* to be afraid (of)
14. 天上 (tiānshàng) *n.* in the sky
15. 看見 (kànjian) *vc.* to see
16. 見過 (jiàn guo) *phrase* have met before
17. 笑 (xiào) *v.* to laugh, to smile
18. 要是 (yàoshi) *conj.* if
19. 怎麼 (zěnme) *adv.* how
20. 說話 (shuōhuà) *vo.* to speak (words), to talk
21. 想了想 (xiǎng le xiǎng) *phrase* thought about it for a second
22. 可能 (kěnéng) *adv.; aux* maybe, possibly; possible
23. 又 (yòu) *adv.* again
24. 家 (jiā) *mw., n.* measure word for shops; home
25. 地方 (dìfang) *n.* place
26. 不一樣 (bù yīyàng) *phrase* not the same
27. 聽 (tīng) *v.* to listen (to)
28. 以後 (yǐhòu) *adv.* after; later, in the future
29. 就 (jiù) *adv.* just
30. 星期一 (Xīngqīyī) *tn.* Monday

31. 小朋友 (xiǎopéngyou) *n.* kid
32. 的時候 (de shíhou) *phrase* when…
33. 第二天 (dì-èr tiān) *phrase* the second day
34. 小學 (xiǎoxué) *n.* elementary school
35. 大家 (dàjiā) *n.* everyone
36. 有一點 (yǒu yīdiǎn) *phrase* to be a little (too)
37. 好笑 (hǎoxiào) *adj.* funny
38. 火星 (Huǒxīng) *pn.* Mars
39. 每次 (měi cì) *phrase* every time
40. 開心 (kāixīn) *adj.* happy
41. 這麼 (zhème) *adv.* so…
42. 有一天 (yǒu yī tiān) *phrase* one day…
43. 回來 (huílai) *vc.* to come back
44. 拿 (ná) *v.* to get, to hold
45. 東西 (dōngxi) *n.* thing(s), stuff
46. 門邊 (mén biān) *phrase* by the door
47. 看到 (kàndào) *vc.* to see
48. 裡面 (lǐmiàn) *n.* inside
49. 一邊 (yībiān) *conj.* while doing… (two things)
50. 看書 (kànshū) *vo.* to read, to study
51. 第一次 (dì-yī cì) *phrase* first time
52. 這樣 (zhèyàng) *pr.* like this
53. 聽到 (tīngdào) *vc.* to hear
54. 回家 (huíjiā) *vo.* to go home
55. 中午 (zhōngwǔ) *n.* noon
56. 一個人 (yī gè rén) *phrase* alone
57. 過去 (guòqu) *vc.* to go over
58. 後面 (hòumian) *n.* behind
59. 還 (hái) *adv.* still
60. 好吃 (hǎochī) *adj.* tasty
61. 回頭 (huítóu) *vo.* to turn one's head
62. 說完 (shuō wán) *vc.* to finish speaking

63. 吃完 (chī wán) *vc.* to finish eating
64. 這時候 (zhè shíhou) *phrase* at this time
65. 手裡 (shǒu lǐ) *phrase* in one's hand
66. 那麼 (nàme) *adv.* so...
67. 一下子 (yīxiàzi) *adv.* all of a sudden; all at once
68. 一樣 (yīyàng) *n.* the same
69. 看看 (kànkan) *v.* to take a look
70. 小心 (xiǎoxīn) *v.* to be careful
71. 小時 (xiǎoshí) *n.* hour
72. 不見了 (bùjiàn le) *phrase* disappeared
73. 聽起來 (tīng qǐlai) *vc.* to sound...
74. 不開心 (bù kāixīn) *phrase* not happy, to be unhappy
75. 不可能 (bù kěnéng) *phrase* impossible (to)
76. 再 (zài) *adv.* again (in the future)
77. 路上 (lùshang) *n.* on the road, on the way
78. 小心地 (xiǎoxīn de) *phrase* carefully
79. 怎麼了 (zěnme le) *phrase* what happened, what's the matter
80. 次 (cì) *mw.* time(s)
81. 一個多星期 (yī gè duō xīngqī) *phrase* over a week
82. 馬上 (mǎshàng) *adv.* right away
83. 怎麼會 (zěnme huì) *phrase* how could
84. 上面 (shàngmian) *n.* on, on top, above
85. 下面 (xiàmian) *n.* below, under
86. 開門 (kāimén) *vo.* to open the door
87. 再說 (zàishuō) *conj.* furthermore, besides
88. 一下 (yīxià) *adv.* briefly, for a second
89. 聽見 (tīngjiàn) *vc.* to hear
90. 生氣 (shēngqì) *vo., adj.* to get angry; angry
91. 不小心 (bù xiǎoxīn) *phrase* to not be careful; accidentally
92. 好了 (hǎo le) *phrase* done
93. 火星人 (Huǒxīng-rén) *pn.* Martian
94. 那天 (nà tiān) *tn.* that day

95. 本子 (běnzi) *n.* notebook
96. 一次 (yīcì) *phrase* one time
97. 拿到 (nádào) *vc.* to get, to manage to get
98. 聽說 (tīngshuō) *v.* to hear tell, to hear said (that)
99. 出去 (chūqu) *vc.* to go out
100. 認識 (rènshi) *v.* to recognize
101. 點點頭 (diǎndian tóu) *phrase* to (briefly) nod one's head
102. 一會兒 (yīhuìr) *tn.* a little while
103. 好看 (hǎokàn) *adj.* good-looking
104. 看起來 (kàn qǐlai) *vc.* to look…
105. 出來 (chūlai) *vc.* to come out
106. 幾個月 (jǐ gè yuè) *phrase* several months
107. 開心地 (kāixīn de) *phrase* happily
108. 第二年 (dì-èr nián) *phrase* second year
109. 男生 (nánshēng) *n.* boy, male student
110. 下一個 (xià yī ge) *phrase* next (one)
111. 沒想到 (méi xiǎngdào) *phrase* to never have imagined
112. 喜歡 (xǐhuan) *v.* to like

Part of Speech Key

adj. Adjective
adv. Adverb
aux. Auxiliary Verb
conj. Conjunction
cov. Coverb
mw. Measure word
n. Noun
on. Onomatopoeia
part. Particle
prep. Preposition
pr. Pronoun
pn. Proper noun
tn. Time Noun
v. Verb
vc. Verb plus complement
vo. Verb plus object

Discussion Questions
討論問題 (Tǎolùn Wèntí)

Chapter 1 外星人

1. 馬爸爸的書裡寫了什麼?
2. 你喜歡看星星嗎? 你覺得星星上有外星人嗎?
3. 要是你見了一個會說英文的外星人,你會跟他說什麼?

Chapter 2 車老師

1. 車老師是哪裡人?
2. 車老師為什麼知道火星在哪裡?
3. 馬天明和謝心月看到了什麼?

Chapter 3 他是人嗎?

1. 馬天明為什麼說車老師是外星人?
2. 你覺得車老師是外星人嗎? 為什麼?
3. 馬天明和謝心月為什麼要去車老師家看看?

Chapter 4 車老師的家

1. 車老師在路上不見了,你覺得車老師去了哪裡?
2. 你覺得車老師知道馬天明和謝心月跟在他後面嗎? 為什麼?
3. 你覺得車老師的家裡有什麼?

Chapter 5 很大的星星

1. 你覺得那個大星星上面有什麼?
2. 馬天明為什麼不開心?
3. 你想去車老師的家裡看看嗎?

Chapter 6 方老師

1. 方老師去過車老師家嗎？
2. 方老師為什麼和他們去車老師家？
3. 方老師和他們去車老師家看到了什麼？

Chapter 7 本子

1. 他們還去車老師家嗎？
2. 他們為什麼想看車老師的本子？
3. 他們想怎麼看到那個本子？

Chapter 8 不認識的字

1. 車老師的本子上有什麼？
2. 方老師看到本子上的字了嗎？
3. 你想一想，為什麼本子上的字沒有了？

Chapter 9 車老師走了

1. 大家知道車老師是外星人嗎？
2. 你想一想，為什麼車老師要走呢？
3. 車老師給了他們什麼？

Chapter 10 水老師

1. 新來的老師叫什麼名字？
2. 新來的老師認識車老師嗎？
3. 你想一想，新來的老師是外星人嗎？

Appendix A: Character Comparison Reference

This appendix is designed to help Chinese teachers and learners use the Mandarin Companion graded readers as a companion to the most popular university textbooks and the HSK word lists.

The tables below compare the characters and vocabulary used in other study materials with those found in this Mandarin Companion graded reader. The tables below will display the exact characters and vocabulary used in this book and not covered by these sources. A learner who has studied these textbooks will likely find it easier to read this graded reader by focusing on these characters and words.

Integrated Chinese Level 1, Part 1 (3rd Ed.)

Words and characters in this story not covered by these textbooks:

Character	Pinyin	Word(s)	Pinyin
心	xīn	心 開心 小心 心裡	xīn kāixīn xiǎoxīn xīnli
馬	mǎ	馬 馬上	Mǎ mǎshàng
山	shān	山上	shānshàng
怕	pà	不怕 怕	bù pà pà
又	yòu	又	yòu
完	wán	完 說完	wán shuōwán
拿	ná	拿 拿到	ná nádào
本	běn	本子	běnzi
火	huǒ	火星 火	Huǒxīng huǒ

Character	Pinyin	Word(s)	Pinyin
次	cì	每次 第一次 幾次 次	měi cì dì-yī cì jǐ cì cì
門	mén	門邊 開門 門	mén-biān kāimén mén
左	zuǒ	左手	zuǒshǒu
右	yòu	右手	yòushǒu
頭	tóu	回頭 點點頭 頭	huítóu diǎndian tóu tóu

New Practical Chinese Reader, Book 1 (1st Ed.)

Words and characters in this story not covered by these textbooks:

Character	Pinyin	Word(s)	Pinyin
已	yǐ	已經	yǐjīng
山	shān	山上	shānshàng
笑	xiào	笑 好笑 笑笑	xiào hǎoxiào xiàoxiao
又	yòu	又	yòu
地	de	地方 地	dìfang de
完	wán	完 說完	wán shuōwán
後	Hòu	以後 後面 後來	yǐhòu hòumiàn hòulái
就	jiù	就	jiù
邊	biān	一邊	yībiān

Character	Pinyin	Word(s)	Pinyin
		門邊	simplified wordstring does not exist
火	huǒ	火星 火	Huǒxīng huǒ
走	zǒu	走	zǒu
門	mén	門邊 開門 門	mén-biān kāimén mén
左	zuǒ	左手	zuǒshǒu
手	shǒu	左手 右手 手裡	zuǒshǒu yòushǒu shǒulǐ
右	yòu	右手	yòushǒu
路	lù	路 路上	lù lùshang

Hanyu Shuiping Kaoshi (HSK) Levels 1-2

Words and characters in this story not covered by these levels:

Character	Pinyin	Word(s)	Pinyin
心	xīn	心 開心 小心 心裡	xīn kāixīn xiǎoxīn xīnli
馬	mǎ	馬 馬上	mǎ mǎshàng
山	shān	山上	shānshàng
怕	pà	不怕 怕	bù pà pà
文	Wén	中文	Zhōngwén

Character	Pinyin	Word(s)	Pinyin
跟	gēn	跟	gēn
又	yòu	又	yòu
地	de	地方 地	dìfang de
方	fāng	地方 方	dìfang fāng
拿	ná	拿 拿到	ná nádào
用	yòng	用 不用	yòng bùyòng
頭	tóu	回頭 點點頭 頭	huítóu diǎndian tóu tóu

Appendix B: Grammar Point Index

For learners new to reading Chinese, an understanding of grammar points can be extremely helpful for learners and teachers. The following is a list of the most challenging grammar points used in this graded reader.

These grammar points correspond to the Common European Framework of Reference for Languages (CEFR) level A2 or above. The full list with explanations and examples of each grammar point can be found on the Chinese Grammar Wiki, the definitive source of information on Chinese grammar online.

CHAPTER 1	
The "all" adverb "dou"	都 + Verb / Adj.
Tag questions with "ma"	……是嗎 / 對嗎 / 好嗎?
Reduplication of verbs	Verb + Verb
After a specific time with "yihou"	Time / Verb + 以後
Expressing "if… then…" with "yaoshi"	要是……, 就……
Expressing a learned skill with "hui"	會 + Verb
The "also" adverb "ye"	也 + Verb / Adj.
Expressing "will" with "hui"	會 + Verb
How to do something with "zenme"	怎麼 + Verb?
Expressing "when" with "de shihou"	……的時候
Two words for "but"	……, 可是 / 但是……
CHAPTER 2	
Suggestions with "ba"	Command + 吧
Expressing location with "zai… shang / xia / li"	在 + Place + 上 / 下 / 裡 / 旁邊
Simultaneous tasks with "yibian"	一邊 + Verb 1 (,) 一邊 + Verb 2
Using "dui" with verbs	Subj. + 對 + Person + Verb
CHAPTER 3	

Expressing "all at once" with "yixiazi"	Subj. + 一下子 + Verb + 了
Expressing "and" with "he"	Noun 1 + 和 + Noun 2
Expressing ability or possibility with "neng"	能 + Verb
Basic comparisons with "yiyang"	Noun 1 + 跟 / 和 + Noun 2 + 一樣 + Adj.
CHAPTER 4	
Expressing "again" in the future with "zai"	再 + Verb
Expressing "then…" with "name"	那麼……
Expressing duration with "le"	Verb + 了 + Duration
Sequencing past events with "houlai"	……，後來……
CHAPTER 5	
Expressing "everything" with "shenme dou"	什麼 + 都 / 也……
Expressing "in addition" with "zaishuo"	……，再說，……
Expressing "with" with "gen"	跟…… + Verb
Causative verbs	Subj. + 讓 / 叫 / 請 / 使 + Person + Predicate
CHAPTER 6	
There are no new grammar points in this chapter.	
CHAPTER 7	
There are no new grammar points in this chapter.	
CHAPTER 8	
There are no new grammar points in this chapter.	
CHAPTER 9	
There are no new grammar points in this chapter.	
CHAPTER 10	
There are no new grammar points in this chapter.	

Other Stories from Mandarin Companion

Breakthrough Readers: 150 Characters

The Misadventures of Zhou Haisheng 《周海生》 by John Pasden, Jared Turner

Xiao Ming, Boy Sherlock 《小明》 by John Pasden, Jared Turner

In Search of Hua Ma 《花馬》 by John Pasden, Jared Turner

Just Friends? 《我們是朋友嗎?》 by John Pasden, Jared Turner

Level 1 Readers: 300 Characters

The Secret Garden 《秘密花園》 by Frances Hodgson Burnett

The Sixty Year Dream 《六十年的夢》 by Washington Irving (based on *Rip Van Winkle*)

The Monkey's Paw 《猴爪》 by W. W. Jacobs

The Country of the Blind 《盲人國》 by H. G. Wells

Sherlock Holmes and the Case of the Curly-Haired Company 《捲髮公司的案子》 by Sir Arthur Conan Doyle (based on *The Red Headed League*)

The Prince and the Pauper 《王子和窮孩子》 by Mark Twain

Emma 《安末》 by Jane Austen

The Ransom of Red Chief 《紅猴的價格》 by O. Henry

Level 2 Readers: 450 Characters

Great Expectations: Part 1 《美好的前途（上）》 by Charles Dickens

Great Expectations: Part 2 《美好的前途（下）》 by Charles Dickens

Journey to the Center of the Earth 《地心遊記》 by Jules Verne

Mandarin Companion is producing a growing library of graded readers for Chinese language learners.

Visit our website for the newest books available:

www.MandarinCompanion.com

CPSIA information can be obtained
at www.ICGtesting.com
Printed in the USA
BVHW050750100622
639222BV00009B/42